"I declare after all there is no enjoyment like reading!
How much sooner one tires of any thing than of a book!"

Jane Austen, *Pride and Prejudice*

KinderGuides™ Early Learning Guides to Culture Classics
Published by Moppet Books
Los Angeles, California

ISBN: 978-0-9977145-5-5

Art direction and book design by Melissa Medina
Written by Melissa Medina and Fredrik Colting

Printed in China

www.moppetbookspublishing.com

Kinder Guides

EARLY LEARNING GUIDE TO **JANE AUSTEN'S**

PRIDE and PREJUDICE

By MELISSA MEDINA and FREDRIK COLTING

Illustrations by LETT YICE

MOPPET BOOKS

Table *of* Contents

About *the* Author

JANE AUSTEN was born in England, in 1775. She had six brothers and a sister named Cassandra, who was her best friend. Jane enjoyed writing from an early age, and even wrote her first play when she was just 12 years old. She wrote *Pride and Prejudice* in 1813, and like her other novels, it's about love, family, and strong-willed women. Back then, women didn't have a lot of choices and had to depend on their husbands to provide for them. But luckily, Jane was able to make enough money from writing books to take care of herself. She also really enjoyed parties and dancing, and she had a great sense of humor. That's partly why people still love her books, even though they were written more than 200 years ago.

Everyone knows that a rich, single man must be looking for a wife. At least that's what Elizabeth Bennet's mother thinks when she hears that a wealthy gentleman named

Mr. Bingley has moved into the big estate nearby, called Netherfield Park. Mrs. Bennet is excited because she hopes that he'll want to marry one of her five daughters.

The Bennet sisters soon meet Mr. Bingley and his handsome and even richer friend, Mr. Darcy, at a fancy ball. Bingley thinks that Jane, the eldest sister, is the prettiest girl he's ever seen and invites her to dance. He suggests that Darcy dance with Elizabeth, but Darcy says no. He seems to think he's better than everyone else at the party. How rude!

Elizabeth overhears Darcy, and everyone agrees that he is a big snooty snob and that they don't like him. Unlike Bingley, on the other hand, who is very friendly. Elizabeth decides that she will never dance with Darcy!

As it happens, over the next few weeks Darcy keeps running into Elizabeth. And each time he sees her he is surprised by how charming and intelligent she is, and he becomes more and more attracted to her.

At another party, people again try to persuade Elizabeth and Darcy to dance together, but this time SHE refuses him! I bet Darcy feels pretty bad for not asking her to dance at the ball!

One day Jane gets an invitation to visit the Bingleys at Netherfield Park. She's excited to go, but on the way she gets caught in the pouring rain and catches a cold. She has to go straight to bed, and stay at Netherfield until she feels better.

When Elizabeth hears this news she walks all the way there through the wet fields to be by her sister's side. This really impresses Darcy, but Bingley's sisters make fun of Elizabeth when they see her muddy dress.

Perhaps they are just jealous of her?

Luckily, Jane recovers and
the sisters head into town where
they run into a handsome young soldier
named Mr. Wickham. He seems to like
Elizabeth and tells her that he and Darcy grew
up together, but that they aren't friends anymore
because Darcy cheated him out of some money.
Hearing this, Elizabeth again decides that she will
never ever dance with Darcy!

Everyone loves to dress up and go to a nice party,
so Bingley arranges another ball at Netherfield.
Guess what happens then? Just what Elizabeth
said would never happen–she dances with Darcy!

During the dance Elizabeth asks Darcy about Wickham, but he doesn't want to talk about it. Jane dances with Bingley again, and everyone thinks they will get married soon.

However, a few days after the ball Jane gets an
upsetting letter from Bingley's sister, Caroline.
In it she says that Bingley plans to marry Darcy's
sister, Georgiana, instead of her! Elizabeth says that
Caroline is mean and is probably just making it up.
The letter also says that Bingley and Darcy will stay
in London all winter so there will be no more balls.

Jane is so upset that she decides to go to London, hoping to see Bingley. But he doesn't visit her even once.

Jane feels heartbroken.

That spring, Elizabeth goes to visit a friend who lives near Darcy's rich aunt, Lady Catherine de Bourgh. One day when she's alone in the library she gets a huge shock. Darcy stops by and asks her to marry him! He tells her that he's in love with her, even though she's not from a rich, fancy family like he is.

Well that doesn't sound like the nicest proposal, Elizabeth thinks. She also remembers what Wickham said about Darcy being mean to him, so she says "No thanks!" Darcy can't believe his ears. Who wouldn't want to marry a rich, handsome man like him? But Elizabeth doesn't care about that stuff. She will only marry for love.

The next day Elizabeth gets a letter from Darcy. In it he explains that the reason he doesn't like Wickham is because he once tried to run away with Darcy's sister so he could have her fortune.

It turns out that Wickham is a bit of a trickster, and Elizabeth now thinks that she was wrong to trust him.

Hmm...perhaps Darcy isn't so bad after all?

One summer day as Elizabeth is touring the countryside, she finds herself close to Darcy's big estate, named Pemberley. Thinking that Darcy is not home, she decides to take a look around. Wow, she had no idea Pemberley was so big! She walks around in the lovely gardens when suddenly...Darcy appears!

Elizabeth immediately
notices that something
about him has changed.
He's actually being nice.
In fact, he is being a
perfect gentleman.

Darcy invites Elizabeth to have dinner with him, the Bingleys, and his sister, Georgiana. Elizabeth and Georgiana become friends right away, and even play the piano together. Bingley's sister, Caroline, however, is still being rude to Elizabeth–probably because this time

Darcy tells her that he thinks Elizabeth is wonderful!

Then something crazy happens!

Elizabeth hears that Wickham has run away with her youngest sister, Lydia. It's a big scandal—what will the neighbors think! The whole family is worried, but luckily, they are soon found and announce that they are getting married. That is, if Wickham is paid a bunch of money. What a scoundrel!

But who found them? And who paid Wickham?

It was Darcy!

Elizabeth now realizes that Darcy is a good and kind man after all. She thinks that if he were to ask her to marry him again, she would say yes. But she doesn't think he will ask again since she already rejected him.

A few days later Bingley returns and asks
Jane to marry him! It turns out he has loved
her all along. He just wasn't sure that she
loved him too, until now.

Jane excitedly tells Elizabeth her big news. Elizabeth is so happy for her sweet sister, and wonders if someday she will get married too.

Then, unexpectedly, Darcy's rich, snooty aunt, Lady Catherine, shows up at the Bennet house. She has heard that Darcy likes Elizabeth, but because Elizabeth isn't from a rich family, she tells her she is not allowed to marry him.

Elizabeth isn't scared of her though.
She tells Lady Catherine that she
will marry whomever she feels like
marrying, thank you very much!

Then one day it happens.

Darcy comes to visit the Bennets and he and Elizabeth go on a walk together. She thanks him for helping to find her sister Lydia, and for paying off Wickham. Darcy tells her that he did it because he still loves her. He says he's sorry for being such a snob and hopes that she might forgive him, because he STILL wants to marry her!

This time Elizabeth says
YES!

Both Jane and Elizabeth get married, and
Mrs. Bennet could not be any happier! Then
Jane and Bingley move into a big house near
Elizabeth and Darcy at Pemberley, so they
can all spend time together.

Elizabeth becomes great friends with
Georgiana, and eventually she even wins over
Bingley's sisters, and even Lady Catherine.

Oh, what a happy ending!

Main Characters

Elizabeth Bennet

is smart, kind, very independent and likes to speak her mind. She doesn't like Darcy at first, but later realizes that there is more to him than his first impressions let on.

Mr. Darcy

is a very wealthy gentleman who lives on a big estate called Pemberley. He is a snob at first, but Elizabeth helps him learn how to be more down to earth.

Jane Bennet

is the eldest Bennet sister. She is very beautiful and always thinks the very best of people, even when they don't deserve it.

Mr. Bingley

is Darcy's best friend. He is always cheerful and kind to everyone, especially Jane. He really loves Jane.

Mr. Wickham

is a handsome young soldier who we learn is also a trickster and cannot be trusted.

Lydia Bennet

is the youngest Bennet sister. She is very wild and boy crazy.

Georgiana Darcy

is Mr. Darcy's sister. She is very sweet and very fond of Elizabeth.

Caroline Bingley

is one of Mr. Bingley's sisters. She is always jealous and sticking her nose where it doesn't belong.

Mrs. & Mr. Bennet

are the Bennet girls' parents. Mrs. Bennet worries a lot about her daughters' futures.

Lady Catherine de Bourgh

is Darcy's snobby aunt and the wealthiest woman in the area.

Key Words

LOVE
Pride and Prejudice is a big love story! Elizabeth will only marry someone that she really loves. Luckily, she finds that person.

FAMILY
Which family you were from determined a lot of things in the 1800s, like whose parties you went to and even who you were supposed to marry.

WEALTH
How much money you have is a big deal to most people in this book. Although we see that it's not so important in the end.

MARRIAGE
Back in the 1800s when this story was written, who you married was the single biggest decision a person could make.

WOMEN

Women are the stars of all Jane Austen novels. We see how women's lives were pretty different back in 1800s England.

ESTATE

An estate is a country house or mansion and all the land around it. Darcy's estate is called Pemberley.

PRIDE

Having too much pride makes you think you are better than other people. Darcy and Elizabeth both learn that being humble is always better.

PREJUDICE

Having prejudice is when you have opinions about people before you even get to know them, which is not fair or nice.

Quiz Questions

 How many Bennet sisters are there?

A. 2

B. 3

C. 5

 **What is Bingley's fancy estate called?**

A. Netherfield Park

B. Netherpark Field

C. Horsehair Manor

 **What is the name of Darcy's sister?**

A. Alabamia

B. Georgiana

C. Mississippia

 **Who does Wickham run away with?**

A. Jane

B. Lady Catherine

C. Lydia

5

Where does Darcy first propose to Elizabeth?

A. In the library

B. At the ball

C. At her house

6

When and where does this story take place?

A. In the 1700s, in a small town in Ireland

B. In the 1800s, in the English countryside

C. A long time ago, in a galaxy far, far away

7

Why does Darcy like Elizabeth so much?

A. Because she is tall and has nice clothes

B. Because she can do a hand stand

C. Because she is smart and speaks her mind

8

How many times does Darcy propose to Elizabeth?

A. Once

B. Twice

C. Sixteen times

Analysis

Pride and Prejudice is a very famous British novel that is mainly about…well, pride and prejudice! Both Elizabeth and Darcy are prejudiced against each other, which means they judge each other before really getting to know one another. People seem to do that a lot in life. Darcy judges Elizabeth for being from a family with a lower social status than his. Elizabeth judges Darcy for being a snob. Her pride gets hurt when Darcy is rude to her at the ball, and Darcy's pride gets hurt when Elizabeth says she won't marry him—again, because he is being a big snob! Later though, once she really gets to know him, she finds out that Darcy is actually a really great person. And he finds out that Elizabeth is incredibly intelligent and charming.

This story is also about **reputation,** which means what other people think about you. This was very important back then, especially when it came to women. Women were expected to look and act a certain way in order to have a good reputation and get a rich husband. Today we know this is silly. Both men and women can have careers and marry who they want. Women have a lot more choices now. Back then, Elizabeth was a bit of a rebel because she didn't care who she was "supposed" to marry. She only wanted to marry for love! And love has nothing to do with how much money you have, but everything to do with how you feel about another person.